LIFE WORKS!

I MESSED UP

HOW TO OWN YOUR MISTAKES

by Sloane Hughes

BEARPORT PUBLISHING

Minneapolis, Minnesota

Credits: 5, © Image bug/Shutterstock; 6L, © Krakenimages.com/Shutterstock; 6C, © Yiorgos GR/Shutterstock; 6R, © stockfour/Shutterstock; 7, © michaeljung/Shutterstock; 12, © Lopolo/Shutterstock; 13, © itsmokko/Shutterstock; 15, © PeopleImages/iStock; 16, © Africa Studio/Shutterstock; 17, © zhanna tolcheva/iStock; 20L, © Thomas M Perkins/Shutterstock and © Pixel-Shot/Shutterstock; 20TR, © Floortje/iStock; 20BR, © nontarith songrerk/Shutterstock; 21, © Antonio_Diaz/iStock; 23L, © PeopleImages/iStock; and 23R, © gradyreese/iStock.

Library of Congress Cataloging-in-Publication Data is available at www.loc.gov or upon request from the publisher.

ISBN: 978-1-63691-945-4 (hardcover)
ISBN: 978-1-63691-951-5 (paperback)
ISBN: 978-1-63691-957-7 (ebook)

Copyright © 2023 Bearport Publishing Company. All rights reserved. No part of this publication may be reproduced in whole or in part, stored in any retrieval system, or transmitted in any form or by any means, electronic, mechanical, photocopying, recording, or otherwise, without written permission from the publisher.

For more information, write to Bearport Publishing, 5357 Penn Avenue South, Minneapolis, MN 55419. Printed in the United States of America.

CONTENTS

Messing Up! 4
All Kinds of Mistakes 6
Being Real 8
Make a Mistake! 10
Talk It Out 12
Saying Sorry 14
Messy Lessons 16
The Art of Mistakes 18
Fail into Something New 20
It's Okay to Mess Up 22
Glossary 24
Index 24

MESSING UP!

We all mess up. Things don't always go the way we planned. And sometimes we're wrong.

I messed up!

It's okay. We all make mistakes!

Mistakes can be **frustrating**. But making a mistake is okay! When we own our mistakes, we know what we did wrong. Then, we can be better because of them.

ALL KINDS OF MISTAKES

Mistakes can be big or small. They can happen in many ways.

Sometimes, we say the wrong thing.

We can make a mistake and get somewhere late.

Even when we try really hard, we don't always get things right.

No matter the size, messing up can be hard. It can make us feel many things.

Think of the last time you messed up. How did it make you feel?

BEING REAL

No one is **perfect**. But sometimes the fear of not being perfect stops us from trying new things. It can keep us from taking on a **challenge**.

"It seems really hard. I don't know if I can do it."

But think of all the fun things we might miss if we never try! Instead, we can be kind to ourselves when make mistakes.

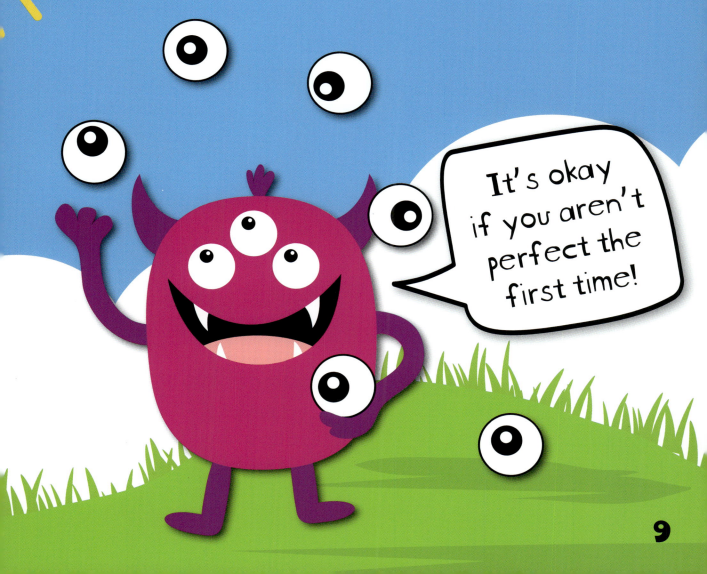

It's okay if you aren't perfect the first time!

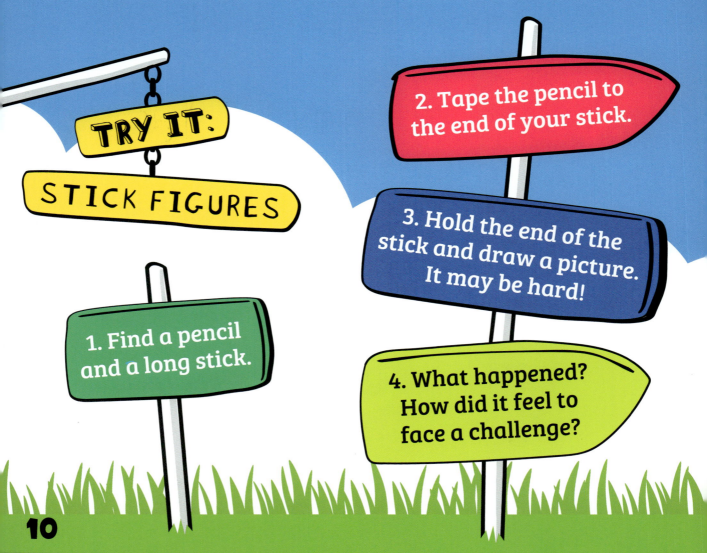

TALK IT OUT

Sometimes, our mistakes hurt others. What should we do then? We need to take **responsibility** for our actions.

We should **acknowledge** what we've done wrong. We can say we're sorry. If there's something we can do to make it better, we should try.

SAYING SORRY

Not sure how to say sorry? It's as easy as S–O–R–R–Y.

TRY IT: WHAT TO SAY

1. **See** it. Acknowledge what you have done.
2. **Own** it. Make it clear that you made a mistake.
3. **Repair** the harm. Do what you can to fix things.
4. **Respond** differently. Get ready to do things differently next time.
5. **Yield**, or slow down. Stop and think the next time something is about to happen.

Saying sorry can make a big difference.

MESSY LESSONS

Messing up is only the start. What comes after a mess-up is the important part!

Maybe we need to do something differently next time.

Mistakes help us learn. They teach us what we need to work on. We can practice those things to get better!

FAIL INTO SOMETHING NEW

Sometimes, our mistakes lead to something even better. In fact, some of the things you use every day came about because someone messed up!

The first chocolate chip cookies were a mistake.

A gluey mess-up created sticky notes.

Plastic was a mistake. Now, it's everywhere.

IT'S OKAY TO MESS UP

Let's own our mistakes. Because of them, we can learn how to get better at things!

GLOSSARY

acknowledge to admit what is happening

challenge a difficult thing to do

frustrating causing feelings of anger or annoyance

perfect having no mistakes or flaws

repair to fix something

respond to say or do something in return

responsibility being in charge of something or someone

INDEX

art 18
better 5, 13, 17, 20, 22
challenges 8, 10
drawing 10, 18
feelings 7, 10
learning 17, 22–23
new 8, 10, 18, 20
perfect 8–9
responsibility 12
sorry 13–15